See the sun **shine**.
It is hot.

Phonics Reading Program

Book 11
sh

Shine, Shine, Shine

by Quinlan B. Lee
Illustrated by Sachiho Hino

ISBN-13: 978-0-439-02027-5
ISBN-10: 0-439-02027-1

12 11 10 9 8 7 6 5 4 3

7 8 9 10 11 12/0

Printed in China
First printing, October 2007
Designed by Angela Jun

SCHOLASTIC INC.

New York Toronto London Auckland Sydney
Mexico City New Delhi Hong Kong Buenos Aires

Mimmy is hot.
She says, "I **wish**
I was in the **shade**.
The **shade** would
make me cool."

Fifi is hot.
She says, "I **wish**
I was in the **shake shop.**
A **shake** would
make me cool."

Hello Kitty is hot.
She says, "I **wish**
I was on a **ship**.
A ride on a **ship** would
make me cool."

Here comes the **shade**.
The sun does not **shine**.

Mimmy is cool in the **shade**.
Fifi is cool in the **shade**.
Hello Kitty is cool in the **shade**.
They **shiver** in the **shade**.

The girls say,
"We **wish** the
sun would **shine**."

Shine! Shine! Shine!